The Coming of the Old Ones

Old Ones

A Trio of Lovecraftian Stories

JEFFREY THOMAS

The Jeffrey Thomas Chapbook Series

#1

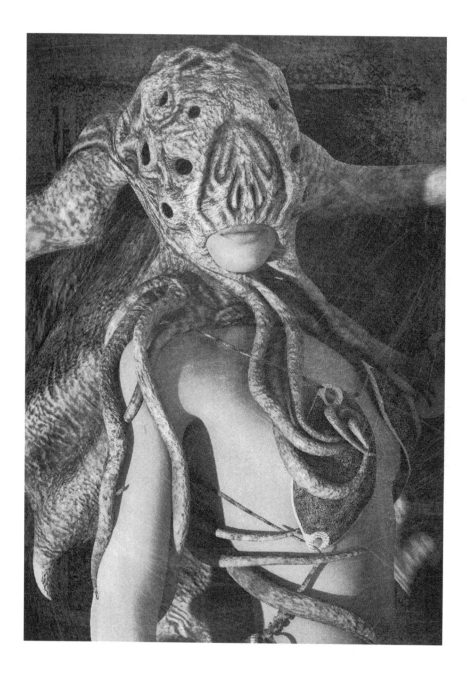

PUBLICATION HISTORY

Around the Corner first appeared in *The Return of the Old Ones*,
Dark Regions Press, 2017.

After the Fall first appeared in *Autumn Cthulhu*,
Lovecraft eZine Press, 2016.

Scrimshaw first appeared in *Through a Mythos Darkly*,
PS Publishing, 2017.

CONTENTS

1. AROUND THE CORNER

2. AFTER THE FALL

3. SCRIMSHAW

4. *About the Author*

AROUND THE CORNER

Coming in from the summer glare outside, the darkness within Unit 3 of the Trinity Village Apartments was like having a black cloak thrown over his head. A vague purplish afterimage, like a negative impression of light, throbbed in the darkness like a great jellyfish pulsing at the bottom of the sea. It didn't help that Franklin was suffering a throbbing headache from having had too much to drink last night, it having been Friday. Though, drink or no drink, these headaches had been pretty frequent lately, for the past couple of weeks occurring just about every other day. He remembered having endured debilitating headaches as a kid, though it was one of the few things he recalled from his childhood.

The smells of the building's hallway, a mix of food cooking behind the closed doors that lined it and industrial strength carpet cleaner, didn't do much for his headache, either. Muted bass heavy music and TV firefights provided an aural complement to the miasma.

Before his vision adjusted to the sudden contrast of subterranean gloom, he detected a low muttering close by

1

like the forlorn whispering of a ghost. Franklin turned toward it and from out of the murk a human shape took form. A diminutive, elderly white woman stood in front of the elevator, poking its button and murmuring to herself fretfully, all the while casting nervous glances at Franklin as she no doubt had been doing since the moment he entered the hallway. One would think he was the first African American man she had ever seen, though that could hardly be the case at Trinity Village. He vaguely recalled having seen her before, but if so he hadn't paid her much mind.

"Not working?" he said to the woman. Though he lived on the third floor he seldom used the elevator himself, even when he carried a fistful of plastic shopping bags from the market as he did now. He didn't spend his lunch breaks in the company gym just so he could ride elevators when he didn't need them.

"No," the old woman said in a childishly self-pitying tone. "It won't open."

Franklin strode to the elevator and pushed its call button himself. "Looks like it's stuck at the top floor."

"That's where I live." She looked down at her two-wheeled folding shopping cart, which was laden with plastic bags of her own, and moaned piteously. "Ohhh...what am I going to do?"

"Fourth floor, huh?" Franklin said. "I'll bring that up for you, but can you climb up there okay?"

"Ohhh...I'll try, I guess."

They entered the stairwell beside the elevator and proceeded upstairs slowly, Franklin carrying his own bags in one hand and dragging the cart after him one jouncing step at a time. "God damn," he said under his breath. He had told the old woman to go first and she kept looking back at him as if she expected him to suddenly rush back downstairs, claiming her supplies as his own. When they reached the third floor he said, "Let's just wait here a sec so I can drop off my groceries. It'll be easier." He left her cart beside her on the landing, jogged down to his own door, unlocked it and left his bags just inside, then returned to the woman so they could mount the next flight. This time instead of dragging the cart he picked it up and carried it in both arms. When they reached the long dimly-lit hallway of the top floor he set it down on its wheels again.

The woman was wheezing and mumbling to herself, eyes closed and bracing one hand against a wall bearing the faded traces of graffiti that had been inadequately scrubbed and painted over. "Hey," Franklin said to her, "you okay, there?"

She cracked her eyes and started a little as if seeing him for the first time. Finally she pointed. "The last door."

"We're almost there, then." He continued pulling the cart for her and forced himself to walk ploddingly to remain at her side as she shuffled along. The wheels squeaked as if complaining after their ordeal on all those steps.

The old woman had begun scanning the apartment numbers on the right side of the hallway as they passed, her face scrunched in confusion. She stopped once, abruptly, to look back over her shoulder, then at a door on the left side of the corridor, then resumed walking. Seeing this, Franklin asked, "Are you sure you're in the right building, ma'am? This is Unit 3. Did you want 1 or 2?"

"I know what building I live in," she groused. "But I think someone moved the numbers on these damn doors." She stopped again, at the last door on the right. "This should be my apartment," she said. "10D!"

The number stenciled in gold on the dung brown door was 8D…D referring to the fourth floor. Franklin knew there were ten apartments on each of the four floors of the three buildings that made up Trinity Village, for a total of one hundred and twenty apartments, though there were one, two, and three bedroom units. His had only one bedroom, as he and Jess had never had children and now even Jess was gone.

"Hang on," Franklin said, abandoning the cart for a moment and continuing a few steps further. Just ahead, the hallway took a 90 degree turn to the right. Coming to this corner, he entered a little dead end. It didn't have an equivalent on the third floor or he'd have seen it, since his apartment was 9C, the last door on the left. This unlit corner had an oddly angled ceiling such as one might find in an attic, and he supposed that was because they were just under the building's roof. The tapered, folded look of the ceiling and walls reminded him, oddly, of paper airplanes he had made as a boy, or of origami. The smell here was intense and unpleasant – maybe from some dish the woman had burned recently, such as fish – and it aggravated his headache, giving it a sharp nudge like a baby kicking in the womb.

Two doors stood close together along the inner wall just around this corner. The nearer of the pair bore the number 10D. The other was a metal door stenciled EXIT. Each floor, according to code, had to provide two means of escape should a fire break out. He never used the back stairs himself, though, as the residents' parking lot and even the trash dumpster were at the front of Unit 3. The ceiling slanted so close to this exit that he figured the door must barely clear it when it was opened.

Franklin poked his head out from the miniature hallway and gestured for the woman to join him. "Here you go, ma'am...it's right here."

"What?" She waddled over suspiciously, perhaps afraid he meant to lure her into an attack. Holding back a few steps, she grimaced at the number on the door as he pointed to it. "That's not my apartment!" she protested.

"Ma'am, you got your keys on you, right? Just try it."

He backed out of the bent little section of corridor to give her room as she drew close to the door and dug a keychain out of the pocket of her house dress. She inserted a key, the lock clicked, and the door swung inward. The woman pushed it in further warily, as if still expecting some sort of wired booby-trap to go off. Meanwhile, Franklin retrieved her cart and brought it to her.

"So...your place, right?"

"It looks like it," the old woman said, but she didn't sound convinced. She reached back and took the handle of her cart, her gaze so fixed on the interior of the apartment that she never looked back to thank him. Her door creaked shut and locked from the inside.

Franklin sighed and turned away, and as he did so found himself facing another woman, standing in another doorway: that of apartment 9D in the opposite wall. The apartment just above his. This woman, though also short in stature, was much younger. This woman he knew for sure he'd never seen before, because she was attractive and he'd have remembered her. He took her to be Mexican or from Central America, with lustrous black hair and oversized dark eyes that were capped with sexily drooping lids. The pupils of her eyes were dilated like twin eclipsed suns, their whites very red, and he suspected she'd been smoking weed though he didn't smell it on her. Still, all he smelled was that stench like burned fish.

When he met her gaze she giggled and he took that to mean she'd witnessed his exchange with the elderly woman from 10D. He grinned and jerked his thumb over his shoulder. "Pretty crazy, huh? I think she must have that Oldtimer's Disease."

"You shouldn't make fun of her," the young woman said. Her voice was vaguely accented. "I'll bet you've forgotten some important things in your life, too."

Franklin stared at her for several seconds. She had to be new here and couldn't possibly know anything personal about him; even his longtime neighbors knew nothing of his history. She couldn't have meant that statement in the way he had heard it. He regained his smile and said, "You kidding me? When I'm her age I'll be lucky if I know my own name. By the way, it's Franklin." He extended his hand.

She regarded his hand as if amused by his gesture, but finally took it and said, "My name's Reyna."

"Nice to meet you, Reyna." He let go of her small warm hand reluctantly. "You new here?"

"We've been here a couple weeks now."

"You live alone?"

"I live with my family." He noticed then how she stood blocking the door, which stood half closed behind her. "I have a big family."

"Yeah, you got one of the three bedroom deals, huh?"

"Yes."

"Reyna?" a woman's voice said behind her. "Quién es ese?"

Reyna glanced over her shoulder. "Sólo un hombre que se pierde." She looked back at Franklin and giggled again, then slipped backwards through the door and closed it. He heard it lock, as the old woman's had done.

Franklin shook his head. "She crazy, too," he said to himself.

A loud, drawn-out creak behind him caused him to look in that direction. He thought it was the old woman opening her door again, maybe to belatedly thank him, and leaned toward the corner for a peek. He saw that her door was still shut, as was the exit to the rear stairwell, but an undulating and amorphous smear of purple light hung in the air in the dark of the corner.

His headache stabbed him anew. God, he needed to get himself to his own place downstairs, take a few ibuprofen and kick back to watch a movie. He knew his eyes were only superimposing that restless purple light against the shadows, and yet it looked more like it was lurking back there *amid* the shadows, half submerged. Or rather, half emerged.

***

A dull heavy *boom* awakened Franklin, its echoes dispersing along his nerve endings. He sat up on his sofa wild-eyed, while the TV still blathered nonchalantly.

His body told him it had experienced a shudder or vibration, perhaps of a mild earth tremor, but there was no lingering evidence to support this. Aside from the TV, his darkened apartment lay still around him. Late afternoon had stealthily progressed into deep night while he slept.

He pressed the heel of one hand into the center of his forehead and croaked, "Jesus." The pain hadn't abated; was if anything more profound. Maybe he needed some food in his belly, and to hydrate.

That boom. He suspected now he had been dreaming. His dreams, he was certain, often tried to send him coded messages. These distorted dispatches from his subconscious were all he had in place of critical memories.

Yes…he must have been dreaming of the bomb. A bomb of water gel explosive that had been dropped from a helicopter onto the roof of the house where his parents and other families – both black and white – had lived together, as the culmination of a long standoff and shootout with the police.

Not that he remembered any of the details himself, despite having been in that house at the time, but he had read of the incident years later online.

In the shootout and resultant fire, numerous people living in the bombed house had been killed, Franklin's father among them. His mother had survived uninjured to be committed to a psychiatric hospital, but had later committed suicide by self-immolation, as if desiring to die in the manner of her husband.

And he, only five years old when the police raid occurred, had been given by his grandparents to a deprogrammer, in whose home he had apparently stayed for several months.

He had no memory at all of the deprogrammer, and his grandparents had never explained why a five year old, whom one would assume to be very malleable and resilient, would require such radical brainwashing. His grandparents, both dead now, had angrily refused to discuss any of it when he was growing up, except for an occasional frustrated exclamation. Once his grandmother had referred to the deprogrammer as an "exorcist." Another time his grandfather, his father's own father, had shouted, "It's *good* the police killed them, before those evil fools called up the devils they worshipped!"

As a teenager, less afraid of his grandparents and less willing to let the matter go, he had persisted, "You'd think the cops wouldn't drop a bomb like that, after that thing with MOVE in Philly only five years before. Knowing what happened that time."

"You fool," his grandfather had replied. "Where do you think the police *got* the idea? They *wanted* that to happen again!"

He swung his legs off the couch but sat there in the fluttering blue TV light for a few minutes longer, giving his heart a chance to slip back into its regular rhythm. It was then that he realized he was hearing another sound that he had thought was part of the TV program that had been running obliviously while he slept. He reached for the remote, muted his television, and listened.

It was coming from the floor above, muffled through the ceiling: a number of voices speaking – or was it singing? – in unison. The words sounded to be in another language, though he couldn't say if it was Spanish. Well, of course it had to be Spanish, right? That was what Reyna had spoken in earlier today with that other woman behind the door.

Sounded like quite the Saturday night party up there. Maybe tequila and weed were the guests of honor. Despite his headache, he kind of wished pretty little Reyna had invited him to join them.

***

Each of the three units at Trinity Village had a laundry room in the basement, and Franklin liked doing his wash late on weeknights when there was less competition for machines. He really only ever used the elevator at the front of the building on laundry night, but he found it was still out of order so he had to carry his overflowing basket down all those flights of steps.

When he scuffed in his flip-flops into the long basement room with its low ceiling, smelling of the underground, he discovered only one other person in there: a neighbor from the second floor named Vondra. Folding the last of her clothes atop a table, Vondra snorted when she saw him come in. "Well, look at this sad lonely man. Are you still moping for that big white girl of yours, Franklin?"

He said, "Nice to see you, too, Vondra." He started loading one of the machines.

"Honest to God, I think men like you would rather date the fattest white girl in the world than the sexiest black celebrity. You see, the racists make you ashamed of your own kind so much you can't bear to be with a black woman. You got to try to show them you're just as good. Meanwhile, fine-ass black women like me are raising our kids alone. I think you must hate yourself for who you are, Franklin."

"I don't hate myself, Vondra," he said mildly as he poured detergent into the slide-out drawer. "Hell, I don't even hate you."

"Huh." She patted down the neat stack s of clothes in her basket, hoisted it up and started past him for the doorway and the steps to the ground floor. "Shit, I thought your big ole Jess came back here to see you a couple nights ago when I felt the building shaking." She laughed at her own joke.

Franklin looked up. "Hey, wait up. You mean you felt that, too? That...boom or whatever? I thought I just dreamed it."

Vondra paused in the threshold. "Yeah, the building was shaking, just for a second or two."

"Earthquake maybe, huh?" he said.

"Guess so. Night, Franklin. Hey...maybe you should come down and have a drink with me sometime when the kids are asleep."

"I would if you weren't so mean, Vondra."

"You mean you would if I was more fat." She cackled all the way up the stairs.

He sighed and wagged his head as he started feeding quarters into the machine. As it started up, he slid more quarters into the second of the two machines he'd loaded. The vibration of the two washers quivered up through the soles of his flip-flops and seemed to spread up his ankles, his calves, like a swarm of centipedes inside him racing for the ladder of his spine...racing for his brain, so that they might start chewing into it and get another headache going.

For some reason, the vibrations made him glance around at the basement room uneasily. There was a padlocked door, probably with supplies or maybe water pipes or circuit boxes behind it, and one window at the far end past all the washers and dryers. To the right of the window, the wall took a turn into a tight little corner. He knew what was there, though he couldn't see it from this angle: a fire exit. It was locked from the outside but sometimes tenants propped it open, no matter how much the landlord threatened with flyers posted on the corkboard over the folding tables, so that they might let in cool air or stand outside and smoke while they waited for their clothes to wash or dry.

Franklin stared toward that dark corner. He knew there was only an exit back there. Not a low, weirdly-angled ceiling. Not a pulsing blob of purplish-blackish light...or anti-light.

"Hello, Franklin."

He whirled around, startled. For a microsecond he had thought the voice had emanated from within the corner.

It was Reyna, carrying a plastic basket of clothes. She set it down atop the washer nearest to the door she had just passed through. It being a sweltering summer night, the laundry room itself like a sauna, she wore cutoff denim shorts and a tank top. With her hair in a ponytail her neck was bared. Oh, all that coffee with cream and sugar skin. Vondra had him wrong. It was *all* good.

The timing seemed fortuitous, just the two of them alone down here late at night; he thought they'd have a chance now to become better acquainted. But no sooner had Reyna set down her basket than a tall, slim man in his early twenties, with short red hair and a sprinkling of freckles, appeared in the doorway behind her also carrying a basket. At first Franklin took him to be another of the tenants on his own, but Reyna faced him and said, "Just put that down right here, hon."

The young man said, "Right, sure, just put it down." He placed the basket atop the machine next to Reyna's, then stood towering over her awkwardly as if awaiting another command.

Reyna smiled at Franklin and said as if in explanation, "James is autistic."

"Oh...yeah? Are you his, uh, caregiver?"

"No, he's just my buddy. Right, James?"

"Right, I'm your buddy," James echoed.

Franklin was surprised. He'd assumed all the people, however many "all" constituted, living with Reyna in her apartment were of the same nationality. Apparently that wasn't the case.

"And he has super powers, too," Reyna boasted. "Don't you, hon?"

"Right, I'm like a superhero." James flexed the muscles of his slender arms, smiling, but without making eye contact with either of them.

Reyna explained to Franklin, "When he first came to us with his mom when he was small, James could recite every word and imitate every sound effect in a Disney movie. But we figured he could do even better than that, so we worked with him, and now James can memorize every word in a book. Not just one book, either, but a bunch of books. Our family moves around a lot, because we do our work in all different cities, in all different states. So it isn't easy to bring a lot of books around with you. With James, we don't have to worry about that. He can recite anything we need for our work." She turned toward the tall young man, who had begun weaving from foot to foot, flapping his hands, smiling toward the ceiling and chuckling deeply to himself as if amused at some secret thought. "James, recite for me from page 984. You know the book I mean."

James started speaking in another tongue, while still weaving side-to-side and flapping his hands, though a bit more quickly than before, and still gazing at a point beyond the ceiling.

"What language is that?" Franklin asked Reyna. It sure wasn't Spanish.

"That's the language of the Naacal people," she replied.

"Huh." He didn't want to admit he'd never heard of them. But it did sound like James was speaking in an actual tongue, as opposed to just speaking in tongues.

"That's enough, hon," Reyna told him, holding up a hand to cut him off. "Good job. He's such a sweetheart. Family is everything, Franklin. Like they say, it's greater than the sum of its parts. Our individual lives are small and meaningless, but united we can have more of an impact on the world and bring about something greater than ourselves...something that lasts where we don't. Haven't you ever wanted to be part of something bigger, Franklin?" Before he could answer – and he did open his mouth but paused for wont of words – she went on, "I get the feeling that you once did belong to something bigger, but you've forgotten about it. Once you were innocent, more open and in tune with the universe, like James is. But you lost that. I understand...it happens to most adults. But there are ways to get back to that clearer vision, that bigger picture. You have to open your mind. That's what our family does...we're all about opening doors. And for you, I think that *remembering* would be the first step to that." She smiled over at James. "You're great at remembering, aren't you, James?"

He chuckled, weaving.

"Well, I think maybe I'm not ready to be part of a family yet," Franklin said uncomfortably. "I kind of like being on my own right now." He didn't admit to missing having a woman live with him. That he missed Jess.

"You should still come upstairs and visit my family sometime. I'd be happy to introduce you." She started pulling handfuls of clothing out of her basket and shoving them into the front of her washer. "I think you'd like them. I'm sure you'd fit right in."

"Yeah, maybe sometime," Franklin said, but he found himself becoming less interested in Reyna by the moment, regardless of her motherly gentleness toward the autistic man. He watched her feed more clothes into her machine. So far everything she had put in was black. In fact, it looked like most of the items in her basket were the same type of long black garment. He gestured toward the next batch she pulled out into her arms. "What are those – robes?"

Reyna paused to look down at the black bundle she held against her chest and giggled, as she had giggled that other day in her doorway. "Yeah. We use them for parties."

"Halloween parties?"

"Something like that."

"Okay." Halloween was several more months away. Franklin remembered the sounds he had heard Saturday night, that he had taken for a party. Now he wasn't so sure. Those voices he had heard speaking or singing in unison...had that been in the "language of the Naacal people," too?

"Wonderful things are going to happen very soon, Franklin," Reyna told him. "You really should be a part of it, directly. Alone we're just like ants, but together we can make a difference that will change things forever. We're all going to die someday anyway, so why not do something of *gran importancia* that'll have an effect on *everything* — something that we could never accomplish by ourselves? Because by ourselves we're nothing. Right, James?"

"Right, we're nothing." He clapped his hands rapidly, then went back to flapping them.

Franklin started edging toward the doorway. "I hear ya — it's good to have something to believe in. Well, got some things to take care of while my clothes wash, Reyna. Nice to meet you, James."

"Don't be a stranger, Franklin," Reyna said, cocking her head seductively. "*Please* come and see me sometime, will you?"

"Sure, I'd like that. See ya around." He escaped into the little hallway that took him to the stairs up to the ground floor. To himself he muttered, "Crazy damn born agains."

Sometimes he found copies of *The Watchtower* left on the laundry room's folding tables or pinned to the cork bulletin board, but he figured Reyna and her family were into something different from that. Whatever it was, he didn't want to know. Despite his efforts as a younger man to learn what it was his own parents had been involved in, lately the more gauzy scraps he thought he remembered of his boyhood the less he wanted to remember.

He wondered how Reyna had sniffed those traces in him. Was she sensitive to some nervous vibration he didn't even realize he generated?

He sat in his apartment channel surfing and almost dozing off. When a half hour had elapsed he went back downstairs to switch his clothing to the dryers for an hour.

He dreaded finding Reyna and James still there, but they weren't. Their own machines were still running. He hoped to get his business done and dash out of there again before they returned. However easy on the eyes Reyna was, he had had enough of her talk of family and changing the world.

As he pulled his damp load out of the second machine he had filled, he found an item among his clothing that he had not put in there himself. Slick, black, and heavy as the flayed skin of some sea creature, he recognized it as one of the hooded black robes that he had watched Reyna load into her own machine. He knew its presence was no accident. He understood she had sneaked it into his machine as a playful gesture of invitation.

"Fuck that," Franklin said, and he tossed the robe into one of her two empty, waiting baskets before he left the basement.

***

A loud scraping sound caused Franklin to jolt up straight on the sofa, to the realization he had fallen asleep waiting for his clothes to finish in the dryers three floors below him. The TV, his only constant companion, was playing a nature program. A chambered nautilus, spiraled like a symbol for infinity, hovered above the carcass of a lobster, upon which it was feeding. The TV's soft murmur explained that a nautilus could have up to ninety tentacles.

Maybe the narration had gotten into and influenced his sleeping mind, because he had been dreaming that his mother was showing him pictures is a great old book spread open in her lap. Though her face and hands were crisped charcoal black, and only smoldering wisps of hair remained on her peeling head, her eyes were undamaged and shone at him both dark and bright at once. She smiled with motherly gentleness at the five year old Franklin and pointed to an illustration of a seated creature or entity with a bulbous head bearing three eyes on either side, and many long tentacles where a nose and mouth would be in a human. His mother had been saying to him, "The more voices that sing together, the wider the doors will open. You have to learn to sing with us, baby. Soon you'll be singing, too."

The rumbling scrape he had heard had sounded like a piano or something else heavy being dragged across a floor. It had already stopped, so he couldn't be sure if the noise had come from the apartment directly above his own, where Reyna and her "family" lived, or from another location upstairs.

On top of being startled from his dream, he had awakened with one of his headaches in place, having seemingly slipped in like an intruder while his defenses were down.

He looked at the time. Almost midnight. His clothes would have finished drying almost an hour ago. And him having to be up at six in the morning to prepare for work. Startling noises, nightmares, and a headache. He grumbled a string of assorted profanities and pulled himself up from the sofa. At least it was unlikely he'd be running into Reyna and James at this hour in the laundry room, and he embarked for it.

Franklin found his warm clothes all neatly folded and stacked high in his laundry basket. Feeling more irritated than grateful, he hoisted the basket against his belly and carried it up all the flights of stairs to his third floor apartment. Having set it down, he unlocked his door, shoved the basket inside, then paused at his threshold to tilt his head a little and listen, like a dog that appears to hear the sound of a ghost its master cannot see.

He hadn't heard another sound from upstairs, but just now he had seemed to *feel* a lingering echo of sound ploughed into the air like a scar.

He closed the door to 9C again and crossed to the other side of the hallway – to the metal door that led to the back stairs. The most direct route to the fourth and topmost floor of this unit of Trinity Village Apartments. He figured once he mounted the stairs he could crack the door a little and peek out, to satisfy the itch of curiosity. Though maybe curiosity was too benign a word for what he was feeling. It was more like a magnetic attraction, though there was nothing pleasurable in the sensation. If anything, his attraction to Reyna, up there, had quickly turned to an almost unaccountable repulsion. And yet, even now as his hand closed on the door handle she rose up in his mind's eye, smiling as if to giggle in that way of hers, the total eclipse of her eyes beckoning like those of a siren.

Having hauled the back stairs door open, he found the stairwell to be completely unlit. Where it spiraled down to the lower stories it was like a gaping well with no discernible bottom. He could imagine the light being out on one floor, but on all of them? Perhaps a circuit breaker pertaining to this portion of the building had been tripped. He held the door open so it wouldn't automatically close on its pneumatic cylinder, the light from behind him all that entered the shaft. He questioned whether it was worth feeling his way up in complete darkness to the next floor. Maybe he could wedge this door open, first?

Then, looking up, he noticed at last that it wasn't just darkness that lay at the top of the stairs leading to the fourth floor. The steps came to an abrupt end at a solid ceiling, with no opening through which to enter the level above.

Franklin recalled then, from helping the apparently senile old woman locate her apartment, that on the fourth floor the exit to the back stairs had been situated in that little space around the corner, not aligned with the rest of the doors in this stairwell. So, there had to be another flight of steps behind the top floor's exit...but if so, where did they come out? And why build these steps here only to terminate at a ceiling? Either the building had been poorly designed or its owners had deviated from the original layout at some point. Then again, he hadn't opened the metal door on the top floor. It could be that, in spite of being labeled EXIT, it didn't open onto stairs at all.

In the four years he'd lived at Trinity Village, he'd never had occasion to go up to the fourth floor until he'd aided that woman, but he must have descended this back stairwell at least a couple of times, for some reason or another. Why couldn't he recall if that were true? Was the increasing pain of his headache muddying his memory? If he had used it, he asked himself, wouldn't he have previously noticed the anomalous staircase that dead-ended at the ceiling?

From beyond the black pool of the ceiling he heard a teased-out, complaining creak. It was more than the sound a foot would make depressing a weakened section of flooring. More like the straining sound the mast of a wooden ship would make as that vessel listed on the swells of an approaching storm. Only the building settling in the stillness of night? Nevertheless, when the creak had subsided he realized an electric shiver of gooseflesh had flowed down his arms, and his headache had ratcheted up a notch.

Perplexed and unsettled almost to the point of disorientation, he let the door close and turned to gaze down the third floor's hallway toward the door to the front stairs at its far end. A moment later he was moving in that direction, like a drunken man trudging foggily in search of his way back home.

This stairwell was fully lit, and he crept up its steps quietly, as though he were a spy stealing up on an enemy encampment.

The fourth floor hallway stretched out before him like a tunnel, as if he held the cardboard tube from a roll of paper towels to his eye like a child's pretend telescope. As he started forward, something odd about the corridor finally registered. The doors on its right side appeared to be spaced at least twice as far apart from each other as were the doors on the left side of the hallway, although he knew there would be five apartments behind either wall. He paused to turn and read the number on the door nearest to him on the right. 4D. He glanced behind him at 2D.

Once again he advanced along the corridor. At its terminus, on the left was the door to 9D. Reyna's place. Opposite that: the bend in the hallway, from this angle filled with shadow like the opening to a little cave.

After 4D there was only one more door before the sharp turn of the corner. It was 6D. No, there was no mistaking that the blank spaces between the doors on the right stretched much wider than those of the opposing wall.

How could he have not noticed this the first time he'd been up here? Too distracted by helping the old woman with her cart?

Franklin reached the end of the hallway, and briefly regarded the closed and silent door labeled 9D before turning his full attention to the bend in the hallway, which he recognized deep inside was the source of the magnetic pull that had impelled him.

As if it had been holding off for him to face it directly, crouched back in the shadows of the corner space waiting to spring out at him like a jack-in-the-box, that same stench that was something like burnt fish but in the end wholly indescribable assailed him with the force of collision. He leaned forward, belly seizing, and rasped out a long dry retch. His headache rocketed in enormity and a ball of silently sizzling purple-black light materialized in front of his eyes.

Nevertheless, he couldn't take his gaze off the narrow side hallway that lay before him.

Three doors lined its right-hand side: the doors to apartments 8D and 10D followed by the metal door labeled EXIT. Part of his mind protested that he was certain the last time there had only been two doors in this wall...that 8D had been the last of the doors *before* the bend...but he was unable to grapple with that thought directly. What gripped his attention more forcefully than the unknown stink or the mystery of the doors or the seething purplish light superimposed over his vision was the physical properties of the hallway itself. Not just its ceiling but the walls themselves now appeared to be constructed out of a confluence of angles so unlikely, perhaps even so impossible, that it pained his mind to view them let alone attempt to contemplate them. It was as though the dark matter of the universe, no manmade material bound by terrestrial law, had been utilized in fashioning this space before him. Angles that were folded and pleated, colliding yet intersecting, tortured and broken and brilliantly mended all wrong...not only in defiance of geometry but in perversion of it.

And somehow, those three prosaic doors still stood amid the chaos of converging planes. But the hallway no longer appeared to end after the last, metal door. No...it seemed to go on and on, funneling toward or *from* a blackness infinite and absolute. And the purple blob of light did not, in fact, float as an illusion within his eyes. It hovered outside of him, apart from him, there at the threshold of the black void beyond the door marked EXIT.

He heard a soft thumping, and a weak voice – the voice of an elderly woman – crying out, *"Help me! Help me!"* As near as a door away. As remote as another dimension away.

"The doors are almost open now, Franklin," said someone behind him. The voice was gentle and familiar. His mother's?

"Right, almost open," James repeated, also behind him.

"Add your voice to ours," Reyna went on. Her tone became exultant. "It's time!"

Franklin spun away without looking back at her, almost blinded by his headache anyway, only peripherally aware that Reyna and James were dressed in their freshly laundered black hooded robes. Having wrenched himself free of the magnetic grip, he surged away from it mind and body, racing wildly back down the fourth floor's hallway. He was whimpering, his throat seared raw by his one dry heave. Reyna seemed to be calling after him but he couldn't hear her over his pounding footfalls...or maybe his mind *wouldn't* hear her. Maybe he was blocking her the way he had walled up the memories of his childhood all these years, as the deprogrammer had directed him to do.

He threw open the door to the front stairwell and thundered down its steps, the sound reverberating hollowly in the shaft formed of cinderblocks. One of his rubber flip-flops folded under his foot at one point and he almost tripped, almost pitched forward down the stairs, but fortunately he had hold of the handrail. Down one flight, then plummeting down the next, wheezing through his burned throat, waiting to hear the door at the uppermost landing squeal open and footsteps coming in pursuit, but so far there was nothing but his own noisy descent.

He had to get out of this building before the contamination spread further. Before it closed around him like a trap, and there were no doors but the doors that Reyna's family conjured.

As he descended, multiple tears began to open in the walls of the fortress the deprogrammer had helped him erect in his mind decades earlier. He remembered now, cloudily, how the deprogrammer had taught him to visualize the building of this structure, then once it was built had taught him not to be aware of its existence, like a desert stronghold lost under the sand dunes. Yet the breaches opening and widening in it now weren't so much random rips or cracks as portals unfolding open in complex ways like the flaps of a paper fortune teller. As he envisioned the unburied memory fortress, against his will, he saw horrible purple-lighted faces outside these new openings, staring in at him. If faces they could be called. Each alien visage more horribly incomprehensible than the last. He could visualize these faces because his mother had instructed him even more indelibly than the deprogrammer. She had shown him these faces in books.

Still, even as these images welled up vividly from the depths of his unconscious, with the last dregs of his self-control he managed to keep his feet moving rapidly under him. As if he might actually be able to flee from himself.

In his blind panic, plunging down one staircase after another, he didn't realize he had gone beyond the ground floor with its front entrance to the building until he found himself in the hallway outside the laundry room. Rather than backtrack, he decided in an instant to follow through with his momentum, and he lunged through the laundry room's doorway.

At the end of the room was that little corner, and around its 90 degree angle the fire exit door that locked from the outside, but which residents liked to prop open so they could stand out by the side of Unit 3 smoking while they waited for their clothing to wash or dry.

Franklin bolted across the room, skidded to a stop in front of the corner where the metal door stenciled EXIT should have been but wasn't, and straightened up frozen in place as if he had been pinned by the purple beacon of light that shone on him. That unearthly glow was rushing toward him through an infinitely long black tunnel, like the light on the face of an approaching train. Its onrushing wind blasted his face, as did the terrible stench driven before it.

Franklin opened his mouth wide and screamed, screamed, riveted there as the wind and stench strengthened and the purple-black light hurtled closer and closer. His screams, though, seemingly on their own morphed into the shouted words of a chant in a language other than English.

His mother had taught him these words from a book, long ago. He had never forgotten them.

AFTER THE FALL

The fossils in the sky appeared after an unusual windstorm.

No weather forecaster had predicted this storm, and its wind gusted across the entire surface of the globe. The storm occurred in the day for those in the United States, but on the opposite side of the world, it shrieked in the night like a migration of banshees. Depending on the local climate and conventional weather conditions, in some places the wind carried rain, or snow, or sand, but nowhere on the Earth – from pole to pole, upon ocean or desert, city or cornfield – was there stillness. The continuous wind was strong, yet not of hurricane strength; it did not bring destruction or damage throughout the several hours that it blew. And when finally the high, ululating howling died down and calm returned to the air, and the sky became clear across the whole of the heavens – whether they were bright with day or starry with night – the fossils had been unveiled.

***

"Are you kidding me?" Wayne's wife said, eyes wide with emphasis. "You're still going to this party with *that* happening outside?"

"Whatever happened seems to have finished happening," Wayne said in a mild tone, his back to her as he reached to the coat rack by the door.

"Oh, and you can tell that? Well, call Washington, Wayne, and tell them they've found their only expert on the situation."

"Tania, this isn't just some party for the hell of it...it's a family gathering for my *nephew*, for Chrissakes."

"The reception after the service wasn't enough? With all this craziness going on, your family still needs to have a cookout? Drink some beers in honor of the guy whose drinking problem got him killed?"

Wayne paused from sliding his arms into a hooded sweatshirt to turn and stare at her. He didn't say "fuck you," though he wanted to. He didn't say he was thinking of divorcing her. Though he wanted to.

No doubt sensing his mood, however, Tania veered from the manner in which Wayne's nephew Keith had lost his life. Instead, she reasoned, "What if in the middle of the cookout the storm comes up again? It came out of nowhere the first time."

***

It had.

The storm had taken place two days earlier, and Wayne had been at work at the time, in his cubicle. It had been an exceedingly pleasant drive to work, marred only by the knowledge that he was on his way to work. A mellow morning in the first week of October, and as Wayne lived in a rural area, the roads were closely flanked by trees that were like atomic mushroom clouds of red/orange/yellow/green, the leaves almost fluorescent where the morning's rays shone directly upon them. The surface of the pond he passed every day was entirely covered in fog, luminous and golden, with thousands of wispy tendrils being teased upward, as if the pond were a deep crater into which clouds had descended from the sky.

But by noon, eating a sandwich from the cafeteria at his desk while he reviewed the quarterly inventory reconciliation, he overheard workers who had ventured outside for lunch remark on how quickly the clear sky had become overcast. In no time, his coworkers' voices grew more animated as they discussed the wind they said was rising. Within minutes, Wayne could hear it himself, whistling beyond the walls, and he finally left his desk for the lobby to have himself a look. He found others grouped just outside the building, gawping at the sky, which was not black as he had thought it would be. It was as solidly white as a canvas awaiting a brush.

"Oh my God," one of the women had said, squinting against airborne grit as her hair started dancing, "do you think it's going to be a tornado?"

"Not in October," Wayne had told her.

The wind had finally driven them inside, while it chased clouds of dust across their cars, which looked huddled timidly in the parking lot. Leaves spiraled in the sky like the tails of invisible dragons.

Yet despite the eerily wailing wind, no tornado had come, not even rain, and Wayne had returned to his desk and his work.

He hadn't gone to check outside again after that. Not until, a few hours later, the gale finally died down...and several of his coworkers, who did peek outside, started screaming.

***

Tania said, "Well, do what you want, and give my condolences again to everybody, but no way in hell am I going outside until they know more about that stuff up there."

"I wasn't asking you to go," Wayne said.

"And you aren't taking our kids, either."

"Are you joking?" their twelve-year-old, Emmy, said as she poured herself some soda at the kitchen counter. "Nobody could drag me outside if they wanted to. You just wait till those things start moving or something. Come crawling down here out of the sky."

"They're apparently dead," Wayne said, regretting he had shared this opinion before he had even finished uttering it.

"Emmy," Tania said, "get the United Nations on the line. Tell them your Dad's got everything under control." She wagged her head. "Jesus, Wayne! It's only been two days! Anything could happen!"

"I know you're scared," Wayne told them. "I think it's scary, too. But until they know what those things are, the world can't just stop, can it? People have to go to their jobs, keep things running. Things have to…you know…go on."

"It's Saturday, Dad," said Emmy. "*You* don't need to do anything. You should be here to protect us if something does happen."

"Your father always put his family before our family, Emmy," Tania said.

There was a time when Wayne would have exploded at that. Asked his wife to explain exactly how he put his family first…what it was that made her say such a thing, beyond the need to prod him, anger him, diminish their child's estimation of him. But he had grown too tired to fight anymore. He didn't ask Emmy, either, just what it was he was supposed to do to protect them if the seemingly fossilized entities poised above the Earth did come alive again.

Anyway, his family was expecting him at the gathering at the home of his sister Sherri – Keith's mother. He was already running late.

Without another word, he finished slipping on his hoodie and went to the door, thinking that if the world kept on maintaining itself in the wake of this manifestation, he would indeed go through with it and divorce his wife.

Maybe this event didn't herald the end of humanity, but a new beginning. He then thought: huh, such a typically human response…looking for meaning where none might exist. Looking for signs in the sky, animals in the clouds.

Just as he started his car, his other daughter – fifteen-year-old Crystal – came running from the house pulling on her own hoodie and grinning wildly. A bit surprised, Wayne watched as Crystal flung open the passenger's door and bounced in beside him.

"I want to go, too, Dad," she explained. "I loved my cousin."

"Does your Mom know you're coming with me?"

"Not yet, so you'd better hurry!" She laughed and locked her door.

In the past, Wayne would have been too afraid to incur further anger from Tania by driving off with Crystal just then. But he hesitated only a moment or two, smiled at her, then backed his car into the street.

Just because this event might not be designed as a new beginning didn't mean it couldn't be one.

***

Along the drive to Sherri's home in a neighboring town, Crystal repeatedly craned her neck to gaze up at the sky through her window with a mix of apprehension and curiosity. Meanwhile, in her lap she thumbed her phone's colorful screen, alternating between searching out stories about the phenomenon on the internet, and exchanging dramatic text messages with her friends. *"It's doomsday, bitches!"* Crystal read out loud.

"Besides that observation," Wayne said, "are there any more ideas about this on the news?"

"Well," Crystal replied, "looks like regular airplane flights are still cancelled, but I guess helicopters and military planes have been going up for a better look. Sounds like the things look the same even if you go up there. Not any closer or clearer or anything."

"So the images aren't inside our atmosphere, but outside it?"

"Um, probably. They're like showing through our atmosphere. Yeah, so I guess...in space? I wonder if satellites can see them. Anyway, I'll bet the government knows more than they're telling. They always do."

They arrived at Sherri's home, parked their car behind others filling the driveway, and came around to her sizable back yard – its swimming pool covered till next summer, if next summer should in fact come – to find that the yard was decorated as if for an early Halloween party. Cleverly carved jack-o'-lanterns on the picnic table and elsewhere, candles in little paper bags stenciled with witches and black cats, black and orange crepe paper bunting, bowls of popcorn, dishes of candy corn, jugs of cider. From a CD player, Orson Welles reported on the invasion of Earth by Martians. All of this was Sherri's work; Wayne had often teased her about being a Martha Stewart wannabe. Mixed with these accoutrements, however, were other accoutrements left over from summer: coolers of beer, and aromatic smoke rising from the grill Sherri's husband Dave tended. He had already filled several plates with burgers and hotdogs. The air had a bit of crispness to it today, but it was still comfortable. The sun shone. The sky was blue...and full of monsters. Sherri couldn't take credit for those.

Wayne realized he was grinning as he crossed the grass toward his sister, who had spotted him and came to meet him halfway. He explained to Crystal, walking beside him, "Keith always loved Halloween so much."

"Dad, we all do in our family."

His sister hugged him too tightly. "Very cool, sis," he told her. "Very cool."

"He would have loved it," she said. Her voice was cracked around the edges.

"I was just saying that to Crystal."

The funeral had been on Wednesday. The day before the event. He hadn't seen his sister since then, but he'd called her to make sure she was safe and doing okay.

Crystal drifted off to talk with some young cousins, while Sherri walked Wayne over to where her husband was cooking. The two men shook hands, then Dave insisted Wayne grab himself some chicken. He'd been busy. Wayne was sure the busyness helped keep his focus off his son.

Wayne glanced toward a cooler, necks of pumpkin-flavored ale poking up from the crushed ice. He remembered what Tania had said, alluding to Keith's death. Keith had been a contractor, reshingling a roof that day, and had indulged in too many beers at lunch. Though he should have been accustomed to drinking too many beers, and the fall wasn't really that far – Wayne had heard of skydivers who had survived falls when their parachutes didn't open – Keith had landed just right. Or rather, just wrong. How fragile, humans. Like bugs crushed in an instant under the steps of vast, unthinking forces...neither of which could really see or fathom the other.

"Fuck it," Wayne muttered to himself, and went to the cooler and pulled free a beer.

His father and mother sat in plastic lawn chairs nearby. His mother's face looked crumpled in on itself, her eyes reddened, as if she hadn't stopped crying since he had last seen her on Wednesday. She had lost her first grandchild. Wayne went to them, leaned down to hug his mother. His father raised his own beer, an Irish red. He'd obviously already had a couple already. "*Slàinte!*" he said.

Wayne clinked bottles with his elderly father, then sucked at his beer. It went down good. It was a good moment. If Crystal had come up to him just then and asked for her own beer, he would have given her one. Not to spite his wife, not even because the world had changed and might soon end, for all they knew. But just because it was a good moment.

He wondered then: why did it often take death to bring people together like this?

***

Wayne had rushed toward his company's lobby, again, to see what all the screaming and shouting was about.

Most of the spectators who had already gathered there were afraid to venture outside, despite the fact that the storm had abated, pressing themselves close to the full-length windows that lined the front wall. But some braver souls had gone out into the parking lot. Because he didn't want to nudge his way through the bodies massed at the windows, Wayne also stepped directly outside.

Like the others, he immediately tilted his head back to gawk open-mouthed at the sky.

The blank white cloud cover had been entirely blown away, leaving what would have been a pristine blue sky like glazed ceramic, were it not for the translucent white shapes that entirely covered the dome of the heavens, like chalk drawings rendered by a brilliant madman on a surface of opaque blue glass.

"Those are clouds, right?" one woman asked shakily, holding onto a coworker's arm. "They're just freaky cloud formations...*right?*"

"I don't think so," murmured the man whose arm she squeezed.

"Is it a...mirage?" someone else asked feebly.

Perhaps fearing they were all experiencing a hallucination brought on by mass hysteria, one of the workers glanced at two men directly beside him and said, "Tell me what you're seeing."

"Teeth. Ribs. Snakes?" one man said.

"Legs...claws," said the other man. "Centipedes?"

"Bones," was all Wayne could say.

The cloud-like images in the cloudless sky were a mad jumble, a tangle, an interwoven tapestry of unthinkably immense bodies. It was difficult, often impossible, to tell where one body ended and another began, even though no two creatures were identical. Their detail was somewhat misty, but still clear enough to appear almost tangible...almost solid, like skeletons lying in a shallow blue pool. Eyeless maybe-faces, spread open like flowers, with multiple jaws or spiral whorls of fangs, reminding one of hagfish or lampreys. Ribbons of comb-toothed ribs, like the curtains of an aurora borealis. Exposed, seemingly calcified organs, torn or exploded, from which protruded bundles of ropy tendrils...reminding Wayne of a dog's heart preserved in a bottle he had seen in a veterinarian's office as a boy, cut open to show the heartworms nested inside. Over there: were those the struts of wings? And there: stag beetle mandibles, or a set of barbed antlers? And those: spider legs, or vast skeletal hands? Had the flesh all decomposed, centuries or millennia or millions of years ago, or had these beings never been covered in flesh?

Fish? Insects? Dinosaurs? Terrestrial comparisons ultimately failed, but it was all the workers had by which to process what they were seeing. Only one thing was certain: none of it moved. These were plainly the remains of expired lifeforms. That the creatures were dead was the only thing that insured the spectators' sanity.

"Come on," one employee said, "someone's got to be projecting these things. Like the ghosts in the Haunted Mansion, you know?"

Wayne heard someone else, trying to rationalize the revelation in similarly human terms, suggest, "That windstorm...someone must have released drugs in the air. Mind control drugs, to give us delusions. Our government. Or...an enemy government."

"Maybe it's some kind of advertisement," another said. "For a movie or something."

But Wayne overheard yet another of his coworkers, who originated from Haiti, mutter to himself, "It's Hell."

A breeze stirred to life, causing many of the leaves dislodged in the storm to scrabble across the parking lot like a horde of crabs. The woman clutching her coworker's arm (Wayne had long suspected them of an affair) pressed her face into his chest and sobbed. But the benign little breeze faded away quickly, and the leaves went inanimate again.

A young man emerged from the building then and blurted, "It's on the news! They're seeing the same thing all over the world!"

***

When the sun went down – no longer glowing through the dense web of ghostly bones, leaving only a pink/orange swath above the silhouetted treetops – Dave lit a metal outdoors fireplace against the growing chill. Those relatives and family friends who hadn't already headed home sat or stood around the fire drinking beer or coffee. Some of Keith's young friends lingered, including his former girlfriend, weeping and inebriated.

Sherri lit the candles in the little paper bags, and the jack-o'-lanterns, of course, which grinned and flickered to guide the dead, or repel the dead, or something – Wayne forgot the original meaning.

The fossils did not vanish in the darkness, but in fact became more distinct, sharper in outline, brightly luminous as if they reflected the sun as did a full moon – though they were lit by no sun of this solar system. Maybe, no sun of this dimension. But in the black spaces between the latticed bodies, familiar stars peeked and twinkled as if to offer some measure of reassurance.

Thick woods bordered the rear of Sherri's property, and a light wind came up, causing the trees back there to rustle ominously as if something huge were making its way toward them. Wayne shuddered, and stared into the restless dark foliage, but the disturbance subsided. He figured a lot of people would be gun-shy about the wind for some time to come. Gun-shy about a lot of things they had once taken for granted…like the sky.

Wayne's father stood nearby unsteadily, and wagged his cane at the heavens as if to challenge the dome of phosphorescent bones. "I'll be glad when a regular goddamn storm comes along, so the clouds will cover up these bastards and we won't have to look at them for a while!"

"I'd be afraid of that," Wayne's mother fretted. "What if they're radioactive? I'm afraid the rain might be poisoned."

"I wonder," said one of Keith's friends, "if we could like shoot nuclear warheads up at them. Blow the motherfuckers right out of the sky."

"They're not really in the sky," another of Keith's friends said. "They just look like they are. They're, like, in some other sky."

"Say *what?*"

Crystal came close to her father's side. "Mom called again."

"Is she still furious?"

"I think she's gone from furious to merely pissed. She just wants to know when we're coming home. I think she's lonely, with no one to fight with."

"Hey, you said that, not me."

"Dad...do you think everything will change?"

"You mean with your Mom?"

"No. I mean, with the world."

"Maybe. Everybody's looking and talking and thinking about the same thing." Wayne sipped his beer. "Until the next celebrity goes into rehab, anyway."

"Yeah," his brother-in-law Dave said, listening in. "If we get through this...I mean, if this doesn't hurt us, you know...in no time we'll all take it for granted like we do everything else. We'll kind of stop seeing it."

"Were they always there, and we just couldn't see them before," Crystal asked her father and uncle, "or did they come here from someplace else just now?"

"I think they were always there," Wayne said. "Maybe always will be, even after we're long gone."

"I wish Keith could have seen them," Dave said, gazing upward wistfully. "He wouldn't have been scared. He'd have been excited. It's really a kind of miracle."

"Like everything else in the universe," Wayne agreed.

"But everything dies," Dave said. "You see that?" He pointed with his own beer. "Even them."

***

As Wayne continued staring at the display suspended thousands of feet or miles or light-years above his company – shuffling in circles to study different areas, like a tourist marveling at the ceiling of the Sistine Chapel – it became apparent to him that these impossibly colossal animals, or sentient beings, or gods had been the cause of their own extinction.

One creature that Wayne likened to an isopod, with a head like the skull of a prehistoric whale without eye sockets, had its jaws clamped around the body of another beast that resembled some kind of eel larvae, with a bunched head like a clenched fist and a crest down its back like a row of praying mantis forelimbs. Another titan that was all spiny vertebrae, with a featureless globe of bone at either end of its serpentine body, had died locked in combat with a thing that looked like an uprooted tree or section of coral, its branches having once tapered into strangling tentacles, its trunk constricted by its opponent's barbed coils. Wayne's eyes were able to untangle more and more of these scenarios from the chaotic scene above him, though the effort was giving him a stabbing headache.

It had been an orgy of killing. But had these heterogeneous entities all been enemies, or had they entered into some kind of suicide pact, having agreed that their reign must come to an end? Determining how they had died was something, Wayne supposed, but in the end it gave no larger answers.

Even then, on the first day, he knew that answers might never be forthcoming for the miniscule inhabitants of this tiny world…which might not even have existed when that epic battle or mutual extermination had raged.

"Imagine seeing them *move*," a coworker said to Wayne in awe. "Imagine the sounds they all made."

"I can't look at them anymore!" another employee cried out suddenly, turning and fleeing back inside their building.

More babbling voices.

"What if they come back to life?"

"They're *dead,* Moira."

"Well, what if living ones come?"

"I need to get home to my kids."

"Shit, why aren't I taking pictures?" This person held his cell phone aloft.

Others' phones rang as frantic loved ones called. Dogs were barking everywhere, as if they sensed something was amiss.

"So what is this, the end of the world or something?"

"The end of theirs, anyway," Wayne said, gesturing at the fossils.

***

Car headlights pulled into Sherri's driveway, then were extinguished. Moments later, two dark figures walked

43

toward the group clustered around the fireplace. Tania and Emmy stepped into its glow. Tania hugged Sherri for a long time, then hugged Dave. Then, she turned and slung an arm around Crystal's shoulders, pulling her oldest daughter against her.

"Ack! Don't choke me!" Crystal cried.

"Brat," Tania said. She met Wayne's eyes in the dancing red light.

He nodded at her and smiled. She gave him a nervous little smile in return.

"Hey, there's still some chicken," Dave said.

They opened more beers. Wayne raised his bottle above his head. "We should drink a toast to our new gods."

"Oh Wayne, don't say that," his mother said.

"Hey, they're the only gods we have evidence of. Maybe that's how they died…fighting over which one was going to be our god."

"Like they'd even care about us," Crystal said.

"I'll drink to them," Dave said, lifting his own bottle. "I bet we won't be the only people worshipping them."

"Got to stay on their good side," Wayne said.

"Aw fuck it," Wayne's father slurred gruffly, cracking a fresh beer. "I'll drink to the bastards." He thrust his Irish red in the air.

All the others lifted their drinks high, then, like a group of irreverent cultists.

Another little gust of breeze rose up, and the black trees massed at the border of the property shifted and hissed, as if the phantom gods were whispering something alien and unknowable to acknowledge those who followed them.

SCRIMSHAW

Massachusetts, 1851

The roar had been going on without cease for three solid days now.

It came from out to sea, but it rolled through the streets of New Bedford like an unbroken boom of thunder, causing people to speak very loudly or even yell to be heard in conversation, causing people to stuff their ears at night with little balls of candle wax so they might sleep, or try to sleep. The roar was so deep in tone it rumbled inside one's body like a vibration, though occasionally there would be overlapping notes, layers of other sounds. One of these was like a sustained blast, or series of blasts, on a trumpet...carrying from far away but abrupt enough to make one flinch. Superimposed over these sudden bleats and the consistent roar, there might be a crystalline ringing sound which penetrated one's ears like icicles. Usually, however, it was just the baritone roar.

"Perhaps it is a snore, not a roar," Nathanial Hittle said to Charlotte, who had early on invited all the ship's crew to call her by the nickname her husband, Captain Grigg, used, which was Lottie. Nathanial in turn had asked her to call him Nate.

"I am sorry – what did you say?" she cried, tilting her pretty head toward him. She had come to see him in his parents' home, to insure that he had fully recovered from the illness he had suffered aboard the *Coinchenn*.

"I said," Nate shouted, "perhaps it is a *snore*, not a *roar!*" Lottie Grigg still looked confused, so he explained, "What I mean is, perhaps the thing is *sleeping*."

"Ah! But what I have heard said is, the Fallen *were* sleeping, but at that time they were absent from our world. When they awoke, they came to be among us."

"It was but a joke," Nate said.

Lottie, perhaps not having heard him, went on speaking with the projection of a stage actress who wanted the last rows to hear her. "My husband tells me they simply move far more slowly than we do, because the current of time they live in is not the same time we occupy. The Fallen are here with us temporally in the sense of the body, but not temporally when we speak of time."

Was the captain such an expert on these entities, then? Being seen by society as superior to the common man – certainly, Grigg perceived himself to be, and impressed that belief upon his crew – was he privy to knowledge that the likes of Nate and even Mrs. Grigg were not?

"So I have heard it said, as well," Nate said, edging a little closer to Lottie so that she might hear him better, though that was not the only reason he wished to minimize the space between them. "Which is why this roar causes me concern. This is the longest yet heard from one of them, at least to my knowledge. What might be only a short cry to this creature – say, a brief exclamation of rage or dismay, or some emotion utterly inconceivable to us – for us could go on for days longer. Or weeks. What if it goes on for *years?* What if it never stops?"

"Oh, please don't say it!" Lottie pressed a hand to her chest, unconsciously covering the vein-shot pendant she wore, and laughed nervously. "I am sure I should go mad!"

Nate stared at the hand she had flattened against her body. He could remember holding it when she had administered to him during his illness aboard the ship. She had offered it to him, soft and warm, her fingers squeezing tight, his sweat transferring itself to her palm as his fever turned delirious. How he ached to reach out, lift it from her breast, and take hold of it again. He murmured, too softly for her to hear, "I trust we would all go mad."

He cocked his head toward the window, its panes shivering so subtly one would need to lay their fingertips against them to realize it. More loudly, he asked, "Do you suppose it is angry that we are cutting into it?"

"Oh, they are so immense, Nate, I scarcely think our labors are any more to them than the bite of a flea. And we have been doing so for all this time. You are too young to recall – they were here a year before your birth – but I clearly remember the day this one and all the rest appeared, though I was but six years old then. They have been here for two decades, and we began harvesting from them more than fifteen years ago, without any objection or opposition throughout."

Why must she remind him of their difference in years? As if she were his mother's age, and not so young, still, and so beautiful. But then, the difference in years between her husband and herself was even greater, was it not?

He replied, "You said so yourself...they are in a slower flow of time than our own. These cries began only several years ago, and they have gradually become louder and longer. Perhaps they are only now feeling the cutting." After a pensive pause, he added, "And if a flea bites my flesh, my impulse is to catch it between my nails, and crush it."

"I see your meaning. Yet even if they are angered, with these beasts being so ponderous it might be generations more before our ancestors feel their wrath...and by then, they will have hopefully found a means to defend themselves from them. Or even to kill them."

"One may hope," Nate said, "indeed."

There was an uncomfortable moment of silence...if it could be considered silence, with that incessant cry. "Well..." Lottie began, as if to call an end to her visit.

"I have something for you," Nate blurted, where before he hadn't known whether he would have the courage to present his gift. "Something I began aboard the ship, and only finished last night. It is a small token of my gratitude, for your great kindness in caring for me."

"Oh!" Lottie said, as he turned away from her. When he turned back, he proffered a sphere, and she took it into her own hands delicately.

It was a souvenir from the harvesting: an orb about the size of a large orange, such a pure white it seemed almost luminous, but this quality had marked it as unsuitable for its potential use. A good orb – called a scrying ball – would be transparent, though with black veins throughout as if it had cracked inside. The milk orbs, as they were called, were only good for breaking down and shaping into buttons, knickknacks, or faux pearls like those that made up the necklace Lottie wore, from which hung a pendant fashioned from a polished oval fragment of a damaged scrying ball. Because of their limited value, seamen were often allowed to keep a milk orb and craft it into scrimshaw. This was what Nate had done, in the idle hours when there had been no chores, no harvesting going on.

Using his pocketknife, and a needle one of the ship's sailmakers had given him, into the naturally glossy surface of the milk orb Nate had etched an image of a mermaid, rising up from the waves so that most of her scaly, sinuous tail was out of the water, and its finned end poking up to one side of her. She was nude, but her long hair covered her breasts. In the background a shoreline was suggested: a sketchy silhouette of the rooftops and steeples of New Bedford, while a few gulls glided in the sky. He had popped out the lines of the etching with soot he had collected from the ship's stove.

Lottie's gaze was fixed on the ball in the palms of her hands and Nate wondered if she had focused on the mermaid's face in particular. The vibration of the roar from out to sea got inside his heart.

She looked up, her expression subtly nervous, Nate felt, but her eyes wide and gleaming, and she said, "It is so beautiful, Nate. I had no idea you were in possession of such an artistic gift. You must have spent many hours working on this."

"I only wish it were more beautiful." *To do you proper justice*, he wished he could say, but his throat locked up. It was already as if he had placed his quaking heart into her hands.

"Are you certain you want me to have this?"

"I could not be more certain. It is an expression of my…my high regard for you, Lottie."

"I shall cherish it, Nate." Her eyes still shone brightly. Had they even blinked since they had first taken in the sphere? He prayed the strange intensity of her expression denoted affection, and not discomfort. He couldn't tell. He had no frame of reference; a woman had never loved him.

Did she love that husband of hers? If so, he must be a different man with her than he was with his crew. There was another nineteen year old crewman aboard Grigg's ship, Dobbin Coates, with whom Nate had grown up in New Bedford. One morning Dobbin was too sickened by an excessive intake of smuggled whiskey the night before to perform his duties, and on top of that in his drunkenness he had spread around a scandalous rumor about the captain. To make an example of him Grigg had punished the young man with lashes from "the captain's daughter," as it was nicknamed: a cat o' nine tails. Grigg had assembled the entire crew on the deck to witness the punishment, and he himself had wielded the cat. This had been during the journey before last; Mrs. Grigg had not been aboard on that occasion.

This most recent excursion of the *Coinchenn*, just past, had been Lottie's first time accompanying her husband. Had he requested that she join him, or had it been her idea? Though a former three-masted whaling ship, usually with a crew of thirty-five, the *Coinchenn* did not undertake journeys lasting three years as many whaling vessels of similar size did. Under those circumstances, one might imagine why a captain's wife would prefer to endure hardship rather than be apart from her man for so long a time. But the *Coinchenn*, a harvester that sailed out only to the one nearby Fallen, was seldom out of New Bedford's harbor for more than a few weeks; a month at the longest. Was it really that she couldn't bear to be away from her husband for even so short a duration? Nate preferred to believe it was that she was simply too bored at home alone, especially as she had no children. Or could it be, he wondered, that Grigg was too jealous a man and too threatened by Lottie's beauty to trust her, any longer, to be alone on the mainland for an extended period?

In any case, Lottie had taken on various duties on her first voyage, helping to wash and mend clothing, to cook, and to tend to the sick. Thus had she come to care for Nate when he had fallen ill and become confined to his bunk in the forecastle, in the ship's bow, sitting close beside him on his sea chest. On one occasion, when his fever was at its worst, holding his hand and speaking to him soothingly…tenderly.

"I really must be returning home," she said, briefly touching his arm. "Please, I would like to said goodbye to your charming mother before I depart. It was a pleasure meeting her."

"Certainly," Nate said, sweeping his arm for Lottie to precede him. She did so, holding the milk orb in front of her belly in both hands as if to protect it from dropping, shattering.

Following her from the living room in which they had talked, Nate couldn't have felt more heartsick to see Lottie leave for her expensive house up on the hill overlooking town than if he had been her husband setting sail on a three year whaling voyage.

***

Captain Simon Grigg had a wharf named after him, Grigg's Wharf, and there he owned a building in which associated businesses rented space. Among them were the counting office of harvesting merchant Charles Bradford, and the shipsmith shop of Joseph Morgan, who fashioned ironwork for whaling and harvesting vessels, and the sail loft of John Mallory, who had prospered by changing his technique – that is, the material from which he made his sails – fifteen years earlier. This large stone building also of course housed the office of Captain Grigg himself, and it was here he had summoned Nate today.

Being a mere foremast hand, the lowest caste of a harvester's or whaler's crew, Nate had never been inside this building before, let alone his captain's office. When Grigg called out for him to enter, Nate found the man – dark-haired and bearded, forty-six years old – sitting behind his desk and moving a circular magnetic block across a plate of metal that rested in front of his scrying device. "Good afternoon, my boy," Grigg said, looking up. He caught Nate craning his neck in an attempt to get a better look at the brass-housed instrument that squatted atop the desk. "Have you never seen one of these before?"

"Not closely, sir," Nate replied, loudly enough to be heard over the roar.

"Come here." Grigg gestured. "Come, come...do not be shy."

Nate approached the desk, came around to its side and saw the scrying device from the front. Its upright circular glass screen appeared foggy at its outer edge, but toward its center the image became much sharper. What he saw was the bustling waterfront of New Bedford, and a denuded forest of ships' masts with their sails furled, seen from on high. A gull fluttered past very close, and Nate flinched, startled. He might have thought he was looking out through a window, such as a porthole in a ship's hull. He knew, though, this was an image transmitted to the device by a scrying ball, fixed in a kind of crow's nest atop the tallest mast of the docked *Coinchenn*.

"See here," Grigg said, and he again moved the magnetic disc across the metal plaque in front of him. The viewpoint on the glass screen shifted, turned to gaze out toward the mouth of Buzzards Bay and the open sea beyond. It was a clear day, and on the far line of the horizon as if painted upon the sky loomed the white double pillars of the Fallen, colossal and misted with distance. "A God's eye view of three hundred and sixty degrees. And then there is this." Grigg reached to a knob carved from a milk orb and turned it with a click. From inside the instrument's brass housing there came the brief ticking of a delicate mechanism, though it went unheard under the circumstances.

Now the screen was a window with an altogether different view: the shadowy, subtly undulating depths of the water of New Bedford Harbor. This view was projected to the scrying device by another veined ball mounted on the ship's lower surface. Again, the view shifted as if a great eye was turning in its socket as Grigg moved the magnet. There was, of course, no accompanying sound to these visuals.

"The gifts the Fallen have given us, eh? This is what we strive for, both you and I, in our own ways. I imagine you have never seen the source of this magic? The brain of such a machine, as it were?"

"I have not, sir."

Grigg rose from his rich leather chair and leaned forward to open a hinged door on one side of the scrying device's base. He pinched the edge of a panel slotted into the machine's interior and drew it out a little ways. It was like a canvas mounted in a small metal picture frame, and there were three others like it slotted into grooves inside, horizontal and close together. Their material, stretched taut inside these picture frames, was white like canvas, in fact, but black veins of various thickness squiggled across the whiteness. Grigg couldn't, or didn't dare, pull the panel out all the way for fear of stressing those particular veins, perhaps two dozen, that had reached out from this panel to its neighbor and created connections. These sheets of material joined each other spontaneously over time, as if mindlessly trying to mend the body from which they had been removed.

"Turning a knob, as you saw me do, changes very slightly the nearness of one panel to another, thus varying the perspective. But the means of calculating such things is more than this humble seaman can explain," Grigg said. "Do they remind you of anything, these fillets?"

"Yes, sir. Our sails."

"Exactly. And we have yet to discover all the uses for the substances of the Fallen. Might we make living clothing from their tissues, that heat us when we are cold, cool us when we are hot, as our own flesh protects us? Pages in books that spell out to us the knowledge of the Fallen, their own living nerves forming words? It causes one's imagination to soar, does it not?"

"Yes, sir."

In fact, Grigg's words reminded Nate of the story Dobbin Coates had shared with himself and others when he'd been drunk, the story that had got his flesh scored with the "captain's daughter." Dobbin had been tasked with bringing to the captain's cabin two bottles of wine from the supplies, while Grigg and his officers were dining. Dobbin claimed he had seen Grigg quickly cover up with a domed plate cover a platter heaped with veiny white slabs of meat. But…if the flesh of the Fallen was edible, why wouldn't that be common knowledge? Wasn't there enough of it to be made available to all folk; wouldn't such an enterprise reap great reward? Or was it, as Dobbin had suggested, that the meat imparted special qualities or knowledge to those who partook of it, joined them in some exclusive brotherhood, like a demonic communion? Grigg said, with an alteration of tone that betrayed bitterness, "These gifts are the least they can do for us, as we are now forced to endure this maddening call." He slid the panel back into place, closed the compartment and seated himself behind his desk again. "In any case...First Mate Denton tells me you declined to sign aboard for our next excursion. Why is that? Have you found other work?"

Nate found it odd that someone of such low status as himself would cause the captain any concern. Weren't young men like himself, eager for work, only too readily found? It wasn't as though he were a more experienced and valuable crewman like one of the four mates who took control of the small harvesting boats, or the ship's carpenter, blacksmith, or even cook. Though he stood in an erect stance before the older man, inside he fidgeted. "I have not yet acquired other work, sir," he replied, "though I have made inquiries." He had hoped to sound respectful rather than defensive, but had only succeeded in sounding vague.

"I asked you why you do not care to sign onto the *Coinchenn* again."

Nate stumbled over his words as he answered, "As the *Coinchenn* sets sail again next week, I fear I am too weak as yet from my recent illness to return to sea so soon."

"Is that it?" Grigg cocked his head a little. "It is not that you dislike working under my command, is it, Mr. Hittle?"

"No, sir," Nate said. "It is as I say."

"Really? Well, you look recovered enough to me, my lad. I fear you are making a mistake. I had my eye on you for better work this time out, as one of the flensemen."

"Yes, sir?"

"Indeed. Think of your mother, Mr. Hittle. She is a widow, is she not? Dependent upon you these days?"

"That is true," Nate said uncomfortably. How did he know? Did he know everyone in New Bedford, and everything about them, like some omnipresent god?

"Then would you reconsider?"

"Well, I..." Nate hesitated. He did as a matter of fact dislike working under Simon Grigg's command. He knew no foremast hand who didn't. But being a flenseman would mean a better wage, if still a minor one compared to what Grigg or even his four officers made. He did indeed have his mother to think of. And there was, of course, the weeks he would get to spend again in proximity to Lottie, though he didn't see how they could interact in any private sort of way as long as his health was sound. Still, just to see her again here and there, most every day…if only to exchange quick pleasantries…

He said, "I suppose it would be foolish of me not to accept such an opportunity."

"I would have to agree. Then you accept? Excellent. I caution you, though, not to grow ill again, because Mrs. Grigg will not be aboard on our next voyage to nurse you, if you do." Grigg smiled as if harmlessly teasing the young man, but it was as though he had just spied upon Nate's thoughts. "I instructed her to remain home this time, after her little experiment accompanying us last time. Even on such a short voyage, I fear the conditions aboard a working ship are too harsh for a creature as delicate as she. Do you agree that this is best?"

Nate wondered how his opinion could matter to the man. "I suppose so, sir," he said at last, probably too softly to be heard over the thunderous growl.

"And her charms, I think, prove too distracting to my men as they go about their work." He chuckled. "Speaking of Mrs. Grigg's beauty, that was a remarkable gift you gave her – the carven orb. She neglected to show it to me, but I caught sight of it nonetheless and she then revealed to me its source. I had no idea you were so talented, Mr. Hittle. Impressive work. I especially admired how you gave to that fetching unclothed mermaid my wife's own face. A remarkable likeness."

Nate's internal fidgeting had turned to writhing, and he felt the flesh of his face burning as if his recent fever had returned. "Thank you," he said.

"You no doubt imprinted her face upon your memory, like a work of scrimshaw itself, during those feverish hours in which you two were alone in the crew quarters. Alas, a delicate thing, that orb. My wife mishandled it, and it fell." Grigg pulled open a drawer in front of him, scooped out its contents in his hands and deposited them on top of his desk. They looked like the shards of a large shattered eggshell.

It was the milk orb Nate had etched as a gift for Lottie, broken into three large chunks and a number of smaller fragments. On the largest chunk, the mermaid had been bisected at the waist, losing her fishy tail altogether. Just seeing this one piece, one might have believed the image was of a nude woman of a less fantastical nature. Nate stared at this woman…the meticulously scratched likeness of Lottie. The milk orbs, though breakable, were not fragile like glass. Multiple times he had seen them and freshly incised scrying balls alike, still slick with slime, dropped to the deck without shattering or even chipping. He thought one might have to throw such a globe with great force, or even strike it with a hammer repeatedly, to bring about this damage.

"My wife was saddened at her clumsiness, and extends her apology to you," Grigg said. "I know you two are quite fond of each other, Mr. Hittle, so I would hope this accidental loss of your gift to her is not too distressing for you."

Nate lifted his gaze from the broken sphere to the hard, watching spheres of Grigg's eyes. "When I can, I shall make her a new one."

Grigg's eyes narrowed slightly, and he smiled again. "Ah...so you are not easily discouraged. A commendable trait, Mr. Hittle. I see more in you than most men would, I think. Yes...I see right into you." He pushed the broken pieces across the desk. "Why not take these, then, and copy what you can from them."

Nate collected up the fragments into both hands and held them in front of him, the way Lottie had held the intact globe as if cupping a gravid belly.

"Talk to Denton, then," Grigg said, "to work out the details of your new assignment. It is good to have you aboard again, my lad. I hope you will come to see me as something of a father to you, and approach me with any concern you might have." Grigg was still smiling, as though this kind offer were merely a joke...a reminder that his own father was dead, drowned after the sinking of his boat when the whale he had harpooned had capsized it.

"Thank you, Captain," Nate said tightly, turning away to leave the man's office. With his hands full, he paused awkwardly before the door's handle.

"Allow me." Grigg jumped out of his seat and came around his desk to open the door for Nate. He clapped the young man on the back as he departed.

***

When Grigg fell into his chair again, he leaned forward with his elbows on the desk and clamped his palms tightly over his ears, squeezing his eyes shut hard and emitting a long hiss through clenched teeth. "*Fucking hell,*" he said. "Blasted fucking hell. You will drive me mad, do you hear? Do you hear me, demon?"

He lifted his head and looked up at the scrying device's screen. "I will cut you again," he muttered to himself. "I will cut you myself, infernal beast." As he said this he clicked the white knob that had been carved from a milk orb, and returned to the view he had been watching just before he had admitted that very clever, very hungry boy Nathanial Hittle into his office.

Lottie was wearing the necklace of faux pearls, with its pendant that was a shard of a scrying ball, as he had instructed her to always do. He could tell because the image transmitted to his screen floated here and there throughout their home on the hill overlooking New Bedford, the point of view of a disembodied spirit. He had ordered her to never remove the necklace when they were not together, and in recent months whenever they'd been apart he had watched her movements on this screen or on the screen of his scrying device aboard the *Coinchenn* more frequently and for longer and longer periods each day.

This was how he had known Hittle had given her the etched milk orb. He had watched them together in Hittle's mother's home, though he hadn't been able to hear them. He hadn't seen Lottie's face when she accepted the gift, but he had seen Hittle's face when he offered it to her, offered it like his rigid cock in his hand. And she hadn't told him about the gift later, oh of course not, but Grigg had confronted her and she couldn't deny it...she knew that he had seen it. Yet she had tried to hide it from him at first, hadn't she, stupid girl?

And she had wept when he had smashed it. *Wept.*

"Whore," Grigg said, watching her activities as if from her own viewpoint through the pendant that lay upon her bosom – *his* gift to her. "Fucking whore," he muttered.

He'd told her never to remove the necklace even when she lay sleeping. Even when she sat to do her private business. Even when she bathed...especially when she bathed. Watching her prepare lunch for herself now, he instead imagined her pushing the pendant inside of her body, and then pressing the pearls into herself one by one. Then drawing them out again, popping them out of her slick oyster in a long slow procession, with the pendant, that veiny eye, showing him the interior of her body the whole time. Emerging at last like a newborn thing.

As he pictured this in his mind, and watched the innocuous actions of her small pale hands that the screen showed him, he masturbated violently under his desk until he rubbed himself raw, and he cried out as he spurted like some wounded and inconsolable animal.

***

The Fallen off the coast of Massachusetts, resting stationary on the floor of the Atlantic with only a small portion of its incomprehensible body protruding above the surface – much like a gigantic iceberg – soared tall as a mountain that had been pared down to two identical bone-white columns. The lengths of these slightly curved, knob-topped pillars were oddly ridged and crenulated, with rows of far-spaced deep sockets. Some speculated they were the tops of two tightly folded wings.

The enormous white columns were hard like bone, in fact, and resisted the axes of human beings. Between them, though, a subtly rounded mass as extensive as an island, also pallid but smooth and featureless – aside from webs of black veins, some of them as thick around as tree trunks – was composed of a softer, rubbery matter. It was at this island of flesh that the local harvesters always labored.

From the deck of the *Coinchenn*, Nate watched as four small boats commanded by the ship's mates moored themselves to the edge of the living island, spaced evenly from each other. They had chosen a portion of the rim that was smooth. The area they had harvested from on their last excursion, on the opposite side of the immense protrusion, was still somewhat concave where it continued to heal. On that side, a thick congregation of gulls salted the island's surface or hovered and wheeled above it, still picking at the great wound. Nate remembered Dobbin's story, and wondered what dizzying secrets the gulls might see and know, causing them perhaps to feast more avidly.

For several hours, the boat crews – a total of twenty-four men, now standing on the island like the gulls – hacked and sawed and arduously pried loose a long, elliptical segment of that white, vein-laced rubbery flesh, as large a chunk as the body of a humpback whale. Over the next few weeks, on regular sorties as weather permitted, similar fillets of flesh would be carved free.

Nate watched the whole while, the masts of the *Coinchenn* towering over him, their sails furled as the ship rested at anchor. Those sails were themselves thin sheets cut from the body of the Fallen, white as paper but covered in a mad calligraphy of ink-black veins, this material lighter but stronger than the canvas sails of old. In his cabin, Captain Grigg could cause these sail membranes to contract tightly against their yards and spars – or unfurl and open wide again – by transmitting commands to them on a machine much like his scrying device. Some of the crewmen Nate had talked with felt the veins in the snowy tissues were actually sensitive nerves, especially since the Fallen never bled when it was cut into.

The only drawback to the material was that eventually time caught up with it and it died and rotted, as did even the interconnected panels inside scrying devices and their ilk, requiring replacement with freshly harvested matter.

A veteran flenseman named Warrick, who would be training Nate, had said to him before the ship set sail from New Bedford Harbor, "Those above our lowly station know more about the Fallen and what the pieces of them can do than they will ever admit to us, Nathanial."

Nate was anxious to begin his first work as a flenseman, but it was more a nervous anxiousness than eagerness. He was all the more agitated by their nearness to the very source of the roar, which seemed to emanate from the Fallen at some point below the water. The entity's call was so powerful here that it vibrated every bone in his body like a tuning fork, seemingly causing the plates of his skull to gnash against each other. Even with wads of wax molded into his ears he feared he would suffer permanent hearing loss. But what were they to do…wait for the roar to subside before resuming harvesting operations? What if it never did? What if it only grew *louder* with time?

The crew had quickly developed a crude kind of sign language, and were learning the art of reading lips.

With Warrick beside him smoking a pipe, Nate watched as buoyant floats were affixed to the hunk of flesh, which was then secured to the four boats with ropes and towed toward the mother ship, the oarsmen working in perfect unison.

Already, a swarm of gulls as frenzied as sharks was alighting on the island where the mass had been removed, as if the flesh below the surface skin was more delectable, more desirable. Until he had begun working on the *Coinchenn*, Nate had never seen gulls battling each other over a place at which to dine. Their hunger seemed to drive them to madness.

A cutting-stage – a platform fashioned from three wooden planks – was made ready to be lowered from the *Coinchenn*'s starboard side in anticipation of the prize's arrival. Warrick nudged Nate and said, "This is it, boy. Be ready to don your monkey belt."

Warrick wrapped himself in his own monkey belt, a wide canvas belt secured to a long rope, and then made sure Nate's was properly fitted. Nate's heart drummed faster, and however cumbersome it would have been he wished he had the broken chunk of his milk orb with him for good luck; the portion with the mermaid's head and human torso. This shard presently resided in his sea chest, near his bunk where Lottie had tended him.

The glistening slab of flesh with its lattice of veins was brought right up alongside the *Coinchenn*'s starboard side. Nate continued to watch the process, but he saw Warrick turn to look behind him so he turned that way, too, and saw a figure donning another monkey belt. This man, darkly-beaded, had his head wrapped in layers and layers of white bandages, fully covering his ears and the top of his head like a turban. It took several moments for Nate to realize the man was Captain Grigg.

Grigg's beard cracked open in a white grin and he fairly screamed over the roar, "With all respect to you, Mr. Warrick, there is no better man to teach our greenhand here than I!"

"Sir..." Warrick began.

"Do you worry about me, Mr. Warrick? I am not yet an aged invalid, am I? And my ears are fortified, sir...fortified against that wretched stentorian roar!" He clapped the seasoned flenseman on the shoulder, then turned his gaze on Nate. His too-bright eyes reminded Nate, strangely, of Lottie's when he had given her the carven ball. "We will both cut into the beast together, will we not, my pretty young boy? Cut into this bitch together!"

Warrick looked to Nate, gave a little nod, and motioned for the young man to follow him over the rail and onto the narrow deck of the cutting-stage. A team of foremast hands made ready to lower it down to the buoyed strip of still-living flesh. Once he had his feet planted, Warrick handed Nate a blubber pike with a long, curved blade. Warrick was passed another for himself. Grigg had a tool called a boarding knife: a long-handled instrument with a long, sword-like blade. This was for poking a hole in a strip of flesh, called a "blanket," through which a hook would be inserted so that the blanket could be hoisted up by pulleys and deposited onto the ship for further butchering before being stored in the hold.

Grigg stood between the two men, and gestured for the rope team to begin lowering the cutting-stage. Nate steadied himself with one hand on a rope, but Grigg merely stood in a wide stance, the tip of the boarding knife stuck in the cutting-stage's floor, as the platform was lowered until it nearly touched the hulking, headless and limbless white form floating alongside the harvesting vessel.

This close to it, Nate saw that the largest of the slab's black, branch-like "veins," as thick around as a man's leg, pulsated rhythmically. If not with blood, then with the thwarted circulation of some mysterious energy, or even with the entity's thoughts?

As Warrick had coached him earlier through pantomime, Nate reached down with the blubber pike and began slicing into the flesh. Warrick started defining the opposite side of the blanket they would be excising from the hulk. Naturally, Warrick's incision was clean and straight, whereas Nate strained more with his implement, doubled back on his cutting, the curved blade veering off course, resulting in jagged edges.

"Here, here," Grigg bellowed, setting down his boarding knife and taking the blubber pike from Nate's hands. "I will demonstrate!" He rescued Nate's uncertain cut, getting it back on track neatly. Then Grigg and Warrick angled in toward each other to form one end of the blanket. The two blades scissored under this squared end, so as to free it to be lifted. Grigg retrieved his boarding knife and stabbed a hole into the strip at this point. A large hook was lowered, and Warrick got down on elbows and knees to feed this through the hole the captain had punched. When this was done, the hook's rope was reeled in and the thick blanket of meat began to curl back, peeling free from a deep but bloodless rectangular depression as clearly defined as a freshly dug grave. With continuous sweeping motions from either side, Nate and Warrick scraped back and forth under the strip to separate more of it and allow it to be hoisted up further.

One of those irregular, higher-pitched crystalline sounds that was like wetted fingers playing the rim of a glass, but horribly amplified, suddenly overlaid the deeper emission. It transfixed Nate as if his head had been skewered with an icy metal lance through the top of his skull and on down through his spinal column, causing him to want to drop his blubber pike to cover his ears, but it quickly faded away again, leaving only the rumbling roar and a ringing aftershock in his nerve endings.

"Ah-ha!" Grigg cried, pointing with the spear of his boarding knife. "There! You see? A pearl for you, Mr. Hittle! For you to carve for my beloved, to replace the one that was lost!"

As if the piercing noise had announced its uncovering, what Grigg indicated was a milk orb, embedded in the floor of the depression. One of the blades had exposed the gleaming upper surface of the sphere. These and the scrying balls grew randomly throughout the Fallen's tissues. What function they served the Fallen, Nate could not say.

They might as readily be needless tumors as critical ganglia, for all he knew.

"Hold!" Grigg commanded the rope team above, showing them a staying hand. He then pointed to Nate and gestured for him to descend from the cutting-stage. "Go on!" he yelled. "Go fetch it!"

Nate stared at Grigg, not having heard him and not ready to comprehend.

Grigg pulled a knife from a sheath on his belt, and gestured with this toward the milk orb below. "Fetch it! We will wait for you! Go!" He made stabbing/digging motions in the air with his blade. "Do as I command!" he roared, because no one could hear him. "Do it for your beloved, you fucking lustful dog!"

Nate turned back toward the thing in the water.

Warrick made some hand gestures to the rope team, and then took Nate's arm and helped him into a sitting position on the edge of the cutting-stage. From there, Nate dangled his legs lower until his feet touched the slab's surface. Shakily, afraid to lose his balance, he went down onto hands and knees as the team gave him more slack. The mass bobbed subtly beneath him in the water. He crawled around the peeled rind of meat into the rectangular depression itself.

He withdrew his own knife, the pocketknife he had used to etch Lottie's gift, and unfolded its blade. Nate inserted the blade's tip into the rim of flesh puckered around the globe, which poked up like the top of a buried skull.

The moment he did this, as if a snare had been triggered, a great maw split open in the depression's raw floor.

Before he could fully scuttle backward out of the depression, the five pointed lobes or petals that formed the edges of the star-shaped opening rapidly curled upward and slapped around Nate's body like the fingers of a giant boneless hand. Nate couldn't hear his own wild screams as he stabbed at one of the lobes, which had encircled his left arm and squeezed it tight. He was being drawn down into the black pit at the center of the star.

One of the five flaps that had seized his body had the milk orb set in it, a blind but glaring eye.

The rope team pulled at the lifeline attached to Nate's monkey belt, and so far this had kept him from being sucked into the orifice altogether. Meanwhile, Warrick slashed at the lobes with his blubber pike. In his frenzied efforts, however, and because of Nate's panicky struggles, one of his blows cut Nate across the back of his left thigh, cleaving it to the bone.

Warrick snapped his head toward Grigg and shouted, "Help me! Cut it!"

Grigg nodded and scooped up his boarding knife in both hands.

One of the lobes shifted position, wrapping itself around the back of Nate's head. Its tip pushed its way into his mouth, gagging his unheard shrieks.

Extending the boarding knife, Grigg sawed at the taut and straining rope attached to Nate's monkey belt.

"No!" Warrick cried.

"It might kill the rest of us!" Grigg shouted, and the rope parted.

Nate went into the maw head-first. The petal-like appendages closed up after him, leaving no visible seam.

"Cut it loose!" Grigg yelled to Warrick. "Cut the tethers, cut the buoys! It is tainted now!"

Warrick, though, only stood dazed and watched as Grigg snatched away his blubber pike and used this to cut through the ropes that lashed the blob of flesh alongside his ship. He actually lay down on his belly first on one side of the cutting-stage and then the other to reach as many of the buoys as he could.

One end of the huge, elliptical chunk of meat tipped down into the water and it submerged as if it were diving. White as it was, it seemed to glow beneath the gray water, ghost-like, for a time until it finally dove too deep to be seen any longer. Whether it had simply sunk, or whether it was swimming deeper with undulations of its severed body, perhaps even to rejoin itself to the Fallen, Warrick and the other crewman couldn't guess. Though seasoned harvesters, none of them had ever seen a segment of the Fallen act in this manner before today.

"It has been appeased!" Grigg screamed as he got to his feet. He was grinning and wild-eyed. "The beast has been appeased!" And he yelled this with all the air his lungs held, even though the roar of the Fallen had ceased the moment the hungry orifice had sealed shut.

The silence rolled off and away from the harvester ship *Coinchenn*. Rolled through the streets of New Bedford, between its houses and places of business like a deadening fog, and up toward an expensive house that stood on a hill overlooking the town and its harbor.

ABOUT THE AUTHOR

Jeffrey Thomas is an American author of weird fiction, the creator of the acclaimed setting Punktown. Books in the Punktown universe include the short story collections PUNKTOWN, VOICES FROM PUNKTOWN, PUNKTOWN: SHADES OF GREY (with his brother, Scott Thomas), GHOSTS OF PUNKTOWN, and the shared world anthology TRANSMISSIONS FROM PUNKTOWN. Novels in that setting include DEADSTOCK, BLUE WAR, MONSTROCITY, HEALTH AGENT, EVERYBODY SCREAM!, and RED CELLS. Thomas's other short story collections include THE ENDLESS FALL, HAUNTED WORLDS, WORSHIP THE NIGHT, THIRTEEN SPECIMENS, NOCTURNAL EMISSIONS, DOOMSDAYS, TERROR INCOGNITA, UNHOLY DIMENSIONS, AAAIIIEEE!!!, HONEY IS SWEETER THAN BLOOD, and ENCOUNTERS WITH ENOCH COFFIN (with W. H. Pugmire). His other novels include LETTERS FROM HADES, THE FALL OF HADES, BEAUTIFUL HELL, BONELAND, BEYOND THE DOOR, THOUGHT FORMS, SUBJECT 11, LOST IN DARKNESS, THE SEA OF FLESH AND ASH (with his brother, Scott Thomas), BLOOD SOCIETY, and A NIGHTMARE ON ELM STREET: THE DREAM DEALERS. Thomas lives in Massachusetts.

Visit the author on Facebook at:
https://www.facebook.com/jeffrey.thomas.71

Printed in Poland
by Amazon Fulfillment
Poland Sp. z o.o., Wrocław